LOVE L

Dear Tinea

Thank you so much for the support

DR. RITHVIK RAI

Hope you enjoy the read.

Kind Regards
Rithvik

XpressPublishing
An imprint of Notion Press

Old No. 38, New No. 6
McNichols Road, Chetpet
Chennai - 600 031

First Published by Notion Press 2019
Copyright © Dr. Rithvik Rai 2019
All Rights Reserved.

ISBN 978-1-68466-971-4

This book has been published with all efforts taken to make the material error-free after the consent of the author. However, the author and the publisher do not assume and hereby disclaim any liability to any party for any loss, damage, or disruption caused by errors or omissions, whether such errors or omissions result from negligence, accident, or any other cause.

No part of this book may be used, reproduced in any manner whatsoever without written permission from the author, except in the case of brief quotations embodied in critical articles and reviews.

Dedicated to that part of us, that once in a while loses hope in love and life and our heart which at times contemplates its own beats and wanders in the quest of finding something to believe and hold on to, while navigating through the beautiful turbulences of our journeys.

Contents

Special Thanks   vii

Acknowledgements   ix

1. The Meet — 1
2. Re-introduction — 5
3. Initiation — 11
4. The Description — 16
5. The Departure: January 6th — 23
6. Afterthought — 28
7. Afterlife — 31
8. The Fragrance Of Love — 36
9. July The 16th — 41
10. Unposted Love Letters — 45
11. The Stand Up — 49
12. Aftermath — 53
13. Lost — 57
14. A Selfish Thought — 61
15. The Dawn Of Reality — 65
16. Anonymous Tears — 69
17. Acceptance — 74
18. Self Confrontation — 78
19. The Decision — 82
20. Privileged Emotions — 86
21. Reality Of January 6th — 89

Special Thanks

Dr. Raksha Kini

Dr. Vidhisha Shetty

Srishti Hegde

Namrata Prakash

Dr. Aditi Santosh

Acknowledgements

I would like to express my deepest appreciation to my father Dr. Mohandas Rai and my brother Karthik Rai. If anything, this is only a meagre attempt to acknowledge the countless number of times I've felt gratitude for everything they've both done for me. A humble attempt to make up for all those times I have failed to appreciate it. Through thick and thin, through my hardships and wins, they've both been my pillars of strength! Without them, this work wouldn't be complete and honestly, neither would I.

Thank you, Pappa and Karthik.
I Love You.

CHAPTER ONE

The Meet

It was cold, the rain pouring down heavily. The clouds filled the sky, lightning striking down as if the gods were angry at the world for some reason. The sound of thunder instilled fear in the hearts of men. Manchester had never seen a storm this furious. I kept looking at the skies from my seat as I sipped on some tea at Jimmie's cafeteria. For some reason, the weather bothered me a little more than it usually does and I sat there wondering why. I looked around the cafeteria and saw people chattering, laughing and sharing hugs and kisses. Everyone seemed so happy and at peace, while I sat there with an itch in my head that I could not scratch. Did I even love her? Was this all worth it? Did I lose more than I had gained? Do I have the strength to go through all of this again?

My relationship with Rachel had come to a point where we had seen the end of our relationship but could not seem to see the end of us. I sat there extremely agitated. The bacon that I loved having here seemed to have lost it's taste, the tea that I was sipping on seemed dull, the happiness of people around me seemed to bother me and I couldn't tell if it was because I was at a bad place or that I was disturbed by the fact that they were happy. I pulled myself together and got up to leave. I kept looking down as I walked and noticed my shoe laces were undone and that's when I tripped on a cane that was kept beside a table. I stumbled and I tried to catch hold of something as I was falling but much like my life, there was nothing I could hold on to and gravity got the better of me and the next thing I knew, I was down on the floor. To be honest, I just wanted to lie there as I had no emotional strength left in me to lift me.

"My cane, did you break it? Did you break my cane you blind fool?" I looked up and I saw this old man, quivering with anger reaching out for his cane and checking to see if it was broken."I hope not!" I exclaimed as I got back to my feet. "That's the thing with you lot, you never see."

"I am so sorry Mr..."

"Dr. Fletcher, my name is Dr. Fletcher!" the old mad exclaimed. He was tall, with curly long grey hair, rounded spectacles and a patchy beard. His voice was deep and hoarse which for some reason I told myself, he must have got from all the shouting and screaming he'd have been doing. "I am sorry Dr. Fletcher, I didn't see your cane, I was lost in thought, I'm sorry." "It's alright, my cane's fine. It's taken more than a little kick by a toddler who is learning how to walk!," he snarled. "Are you all right, or have you hurt yourself?" he added. "I'm alright sir," I replied. "Good, now get out of my sight!" he exclaimed and went back to his seat and began writing in his diary. As I walked out of the cafeteria, I had one last look at the old man sitting there, mumbling to himself and writing. For some reason, the whole incident brought a weird smile to my face. It was when I reached home that I realised that I had left my umbrella back at the cafeteria and I was soaking wet from the rain. "You really are lost in thought, aren't you, Sam?" I told myself.

Later that night, I sat there, in front of the fire place just staring into the flames and the whole house seemed so silent. It was almost as if the whole universe had turned down its volume to listen to my thoughts. My dad was away visiting my grandmother, his mother, as she was unwell. I refused to go along as I wasn't very good with dealing with emotional situations. My family pretty much consisted of just me and my dad. My mother had passed away when I was very little and I had very few memories of her. Back then, I was too young to find out how she passed away and now I guess I'm too afraid to know the answer. I sat there contemplating my decisions in life. I could feel my heart pounding. I was not sure if it was because of my concern for my grandmother or the fact that I was about to start med school in a few weeks or that I had no clue what was going on in Rachel's mind.

Rachel and I were together for about 4 years and in those 4 years, we had really stretched the fabric of our relationship and it had gone from lust, to love, to anger, to hatred.

Emotions are just like seasons. They change over time, and we will feel them again after a period of time but when will that time come? That's a question always left unanswered. My mind ran through multiple emotions that night unwilling to stop, refusing to rest. It felt like my mind was about to explode. I was so confused and for the most part, I was not sure why. "It's time to go, Sam," a voice called out to me and I looked up and saw Rachel standing by the door. There she was, so perfect with all her imperfections. Her long black hair falling all the way down to her waist, that smile that made my heart skip a beat every time I saw it, and that perfect streak of hair falling in front of her eyes which she then gently slipped behind her ear. I got up and we left. We drove into the night, not uttering a single word to each other. She just sat there lost in the words of our favourite song that was playing on the radio, 'with or without you,' by U2 and I looked across and saw her next to me with her eyes closed and right at that moment, I felt like I had instantly fallen in love all over again. We finally reached home and I looked at her with tears in my eyes. "Why the tears, Sam?" she asked, gently wiping them off. "We finally made it. After all that we've been through, we are finally here and you are here next to me and every time I think of this, it makes me feel like I've got all that I've ever wanted, right here," I told her with a weak voice. "Well we made it.," she replied with a smile gently pinching my arm like she always did, but this time it felt different. For some reason, it hurt a lot and that's when I began to wonder, where had we come? Why did it feel so unfamiliar even though it felt like home? I looked at her and she started to blur out. I tried hard to keep focusing on her smile, but for some reason I just couldn't get a hold of myself and then I opened my eyes and found myself lying on my bed all alone. I looked to my left and saw nothing but an empty half of the bed and I told myself with a helpless smile on my face, "if only," and tried to go back to sleep. Somehow I managed through the night with struggling emotions and thoughts, like most of us do, every night, for most nights in one way or the other.

CHAPTER TWO

Re-Introduction

I woke up the next day to the sound of roaring thunder. I stepped out to my balcony and saw the clouds fill the morning sky. The thunder continued to rumble as I took in a deep breath of fresh air and let it fill my lungs. I felt good. My emotions felt new and, though I knew that it wouldn't last long, I was satisfied. I made myself a nice plate of scrambled eggs and toast and a cup of tea as that was the only thing I was capable of cooking and I headed out for my morning walk. I took a long walk to the Carmile Bridge. I stood there looking down at the water droplets dancing on the surface of the river. This bridge always took me back to the first time Rachel and I felt like we experienced a piece of our souls. It was back when my grand dad had just passed away and I was heartbroken. I had spent most of my childhood summers with him. He would take me to this park every night and tell me, "Look up at the stars every night Sammy, and remind yourself that you too, are one. You are filled with fire, determination, rage, outshining the darkness with the light that radiates from within!"

The day I heard that he was no more, I refused to even go to the funeral. I do regret my decision sometimes, but I guess I just didn't have the strength to see his lifeless form after that.

I had stood right here 4 years back and it seems like it was just yesterday. "Sam, what are you doing here? I've been looking everywhere for you, I've been worried sick!" Rachel screamed. I just stood there, the lightning striking the ground, far away in the horizon and yet I didn't care. The rain was pouring down with all its fury. She kept pulling me by my shirt, trying to drag me away.

"Tell me Rachel, can you see my tears?" I asked her.

"Come let's go before you fall sick!" she shouted trying to pull me away, to get me to start walking. I held both her arms and looked into her eyes and asked; "Now you know why I love the rain so much!" We just stood there looking into each other's eyes and then I fell to my knees, as if my legs had lost all their strength and I could not seem to be able to get back up. "I don't have the strength to fight this alone Rachel, I just don't. I don't want to live like this, afraid every single night, wondering who I am going to lose next!," I exclaimed. She sat down with me and looked into my eyes and said, "I may not be able to stop you from being hurt, because pain, my darling, is inevitable; but what I can promise you is that you will never be hurting alone. And to answer your question Sam, yes, I can see your tears, I could see them even when you had no tears in your eyes and that's why I am drawn to you!" It was at that moment, right there, for the first time I felt warm, even though we were drenched and cold, I felt the warmth, and to this day, I feel warm when I think of her and I ask myself,' Where did we go wrong?.'

The thunder continued to rumble and I started to walk back. I spent most of my morning and noon catching up with old friends, talking about college and all the memories we had made over the past few years. It was our last few weeks together before we left for different destinations. That evening, I went back to Jimmie's cafeteria, to have some bacon. It's like they say, old habits die hard and no matter how dull it tasted, and I just couldn't stop having it irrespective of how it made me feel anymore. I entered into a jam packed cafeteria and it felt the same. Same happy people with their laughers and giggles. It disgusted me. I ordered my bacons to go and as I was waiting for my food, I looked around and saw the same old man, with his cane, sitting at a corner of the room, looking out of the window and staring into the space. For some reason, I felt like approaching him and talking to him.

"Hello Dr. Fletcher, we met yesterday right here if you remember," I told him with a smile. He looked up and asked, "Did we?" in a soft voice. For a moment, I was confused, as to if it was the same Dr. Fletcher who had yelled at me the previous day and I said, "Err yes sir, I tripped over your cane yesterday."

"Ah yes, yes, of course, I remember now boy; have a seat," he said pointing to the seat in front of him. "Thank you very much sir, I am Sam Gray," I told him as I sat down. "That's a wonderful name, I love it," he exclaimed. I was still a bit confused wondering if it was the same rude man I had met yesterday. "I see that you have curly hair just like mine, only yours is all black and mine has aged like fine wine!" he exclaimed with a smile. I laughed and it felt good sitting there with this stranger. Maybe I was missing my granddad a little too much today and maybe that's why I tried to have a conversation with him.

"I am sorry Dr. Fletcher, I was just waiting for my food and I noticed that you were sitting here all by yourself and for some reason, I'm missing my granddad a lot today and

you kind of reminded me of him and so I came to say hello."
"He passed away about 4 years ago and I really miss him" I added.

"Death is defined in our dictionaries as, 'The end of the life of a person or an organism'; stating that you are dead when your brain, heart and lungs cease to function. Humanity has so easily pinned down such terminologies and tried to show the world, that if you are not dead, then you are alive!" he exclaimed. "As it's said, the greatest trick the devil ever played was making the world believe that he does not exist" he added. "Tell me, do you think death actually is the final word?" he asked me, staring at me eagerly waiting for an answer. "Err, yes I think so," I replied clearing my throat. "Then why do you miss him?" he asked with a loud voice. I was stuck, for a moment there, I really began to wonder. "Ha!" he exclaimed with a wide smile. "Tell me, why do you miss him then? I'll tell you why, it's because we all try to find meaning in sadness, misery and pain, like it's some sacred road to salvation. Some of us choose the path of happiness, wherein, we try to make ourselves and the people around us happy and live a decent journey. Is it because we crave it, or is it because we are too afraid of pain?

What if, love, hatred, life and death, are actually physical quantities like time, distance and speed, which we, as humans, have not yet learnt to quantify, and hence have chosen to live such lives. This son is the essence of life" he added. "The essence of life is not life itself, but the fragrance of it. It's not the moment itself, but rather the thoughts and works leading to it and remaining with us afterwards. It's not all flesh and blood but rather the memories of the past and the vision of the future we keep with us. That's why emotions run deeper than they did, once the moment has passed. If you feel closely with your eyes closed, you'll realise that the thoughts of the moment gives us more happiness than the moment itself and that's why in the end, that is what gives us the essence of life and the fragrance of life never dies and goes on forever." I was in a state of shock when I heard this. This man in front of me, with such simple words, he had explained to me the meaning of life and my mind was blown. I was unable to digest the lines he was telling me. The world around me seemed to not bother me anymore. The voices of the people around me faded. I could hear nothing but his words. I was speechless. "Ha, I got you good didn't I boy!" he exclaimed. It took me a while to get a few words from my brain to the tip of my tongue, "Yes, yes sir, you sure did," I replied.

"Sam Gray," a voiced called out. It was the lady at the counter; my food was ready. "It's a beautiful perspective you have there Dr. Fletcher," I told him with a smile. "Of course I do boy, when u have lived the life I have lived, your ideals and perspectives are going to be brilliant," he replied with a grin. Dr. Fletcher had a weird sense of humour, but I thought I was slowly getting the hang of it. "I'd love to hear more of your views and stories sir," I told him, hoping he would not ask me to get lost again. "I'd love to," he replied to my surprise, with a smile. The evenings get lonely here. "I've been coming here often, it helps me, they say." "Me too" I exclaimed with excitement. "It's a wonder how I haven't noticed you all this while." "I'll tell you why son" he replied signalling me to come closer. I leaned in and he whispered into my ears, "We are more self-involved than you think we are!" he whispered and then began to laugh. I couldn't help but laugh along. "Sam Gray," the lady at the counter called again. "Sam Gray, tall, lean, 5 ft. 10 inches

I'd say, curly hair, more lost than he thinks he is, sweet smile, round face, probably would look better with glasses I'd say," he began describing me as he wrote it down in his book. "What's that for Dr. Fletcher?" I asked. "Oh nothing, just some casual mental exercise," he replied. "Sam Gray!" the lady at the counter shouted a bit louder this time. I could sense that she was losing her patience. "OK sir, I think I'd better leave, I'll talk to you tomorrow, and it's been a pleasure." "The pleasure's mine boy," he replied waving goodbye. I collected my food and as I was exiting, I turned to look at him and he had already begun writing, mumbling to himself again. I walked out of the cafeteria feeling much better than I did when I had entered it. I felt like I had met a powerful mind who with just few words had got me pretty much thinking about life in a whole new perspective. I just couldn't wait to meet him again the next day. Once I reached home, I gave my dad a call and enquired about my grand mom. He informed me that she wasn't doing too well and he insisted that I pay her a visit. I refused again, as these were some of the skeletons in my closet I was still fighting and wasn't strong enough to face. I spent the rest of my night, looking at pictures of my granddad and I from the old family albums and it really filled my heart with joy.

CHAPTER THREE

Initiation

The next day, I woke up feeling much better than I did in the past couple of days. I was really excited to go back to the cafeteria and meet Dr. Fletcher in the evening. I sat and thought of all the things we could speak about. His words excited me a lot. A Strange man, I would say, completely unpredictable. As I sat in my living room, I thought that I should clean my room for a change. My dad would always nag and say 'A man with messy habits ends being messy in life.' I would always reply by saying, 'All smart men are messy,' and laugh it off, ignoring his statements. But looking at the state I was in, I guess he was right. I entered my room and for the first time I noticed how big of a mess it really was. Picture a room if you left 3 cats and 3 dogs with 5 mice and you locked the door for a good 10 minutes. That's what my room looked like. I began to place my books back on the shelf and as I looked over the shelf, I saw a crumpled piece of paper at the back. I tried to think of what it might be, but I was absolutely clueless and so I reached out and grabbed it, curious to find out what it was.

"I am the one who writes these words
But it's my heart that speaks
What do I do?
I am silent
Only because she wants to hear my heart
Not my words
If I oblige,
Then these words from my heart would have no end
These tears would never stop
This love of mine, would be a weakness
This pain would have been so hard to endure
But what can I do?
I am in search of her
But she is in search of my heart
How do I define what I feel?
I'm unable to erase it, unable to break it
I speak, but there is no voice
There are no words, but there's no silence
What do I say? What can I say?
After all, words are just words!"

I stood there, staring at this piece of paper I was holding and my hands began to tremble. This is what I had for her. Where did I lose all these emotions? Dr. Fletcher's words began to echo in my mind of how people are more self-involved than they actually think they are. How could we have lost what we had? I sat on my bed and tried to think of what had happened between us. She never complained of anything. I had never asked her to change; I was never the possessive kind. Always gave her space and spoke to her with respect. I never mistreated her. I fell flat on my back and looked up at the ceiling and the past came screaming back to me. "Why don't you get it Sam?" Rachel screamed.

"Get what? What do you want me to understand, I don't get what the problem is!" I exclaimed. "You never get what the problem is! You always want things to be explained to you. Everything has to be made easy for you. You are not a child, for me to have to sit and simplify things for you every single time," she shouted. "Just talk to me, tell me what you want?" I said, in a soft voice. "I want you!" she shouted. "But you have me," I said with a smile. "Yes I do! I have your time, you are always there for me, I have your respect, I have your non-jealous attitude and I have your annoying sense of humour that you use as a shield!" she shouted, being even louder this time. Her voice got louder every minute and mine, softer. "What more do you want Rach?" I asked. "I want your emotional investment Sam! I want you to let me be there for you as much as you are for me. I want to be the person you come crawling to when you are hurt like the first time you did, back at the bridge. I want to know that you need me, as much as I need you." she said, crying this time. I walked up to her and gently wiped her tears and said, "There are two kinds of people in this world my darling, one who survives and the other who lives. I am a man who is just surviving, but with you my darling, I live. When I pick you up and dust you off, I feel like I'm beginning to live a little more than I did yesterday. But one thing I realised is that you are not as strong as I am. You haven't been through the things that I have been through and if I let you in any more than I already have, it will break you just as it broke me," I said, gently caressing her hair. "Tell me, isn't it better that you live completely and me partly from your happiness than the both of us just surviving because honestly my darling, I can never let go of my past, and my past is my present and it will be my future and it makes me who I am and I am not willing to let go of it," I added. "Then you'll have to let go of me!," she shouted pushing me to the ground. I sat there smiling helplessly for some weird reason. I pulled myself up and held her by her hands and said, "Okay."

"Ok? Ok? Are you fucking letting me go because I asked you to? Fight for me Sam, fight for us. Look me in the eye and tell me that you love me, that you want me." She said pulling me by the collar. "I do want you, and you know that I love you more than I love myself. All this while I felt that I was reducing your burden by always being there for you, but now I feel that I've become a burden to you, and to be honest, I'm too heavy a weight to carry," I told her, gently trying to release her grip off my shirt. "Stay with me Sam, stay!" she shouted.

"Ok, I will. Anything for you," I replied having freed myself from her grip.

"Argh, Sam! You just don't get it!" she exclaimed, as she turned and stormed out.

I remember vividly that she turned around with so much frustration that the ends of her hair hit my face and as she walked away, I remember telling myself, 'You love her so much, but why is that your legs go numb and your words get stuck in your throat and all you can do is watch her walk away.' I came back home that day and wrote all that I felt on a piece of paper and crumpled it and threw it away only to find it today.

That evening, I headed to Jimmie's and I just could not get Rachel out of my head through the entire walk. As I entered the cafeteria, I saw Dr. Fletcher at the same spot. I walked up to him and sat down and asked, "Tell me Dr. Fletcher, why is being in love such a pain in the ass?" He just sat there smiling. I was waiting for him to answer me even though I was not looking for an answer as I had already convinced myself that love was nothing but a dreadful bond. He took a deep breath, "Is it the 16th of July?" he asked. I looked at my watch and replied, "No sir, it's the 13th." "Ah, so it's nearing, I can already smell her fragrance in the air, can't you!" he exclaimed. "Who sir? What fragrance?" I asked confused.

"EV!" he exclaimed, "Emma Veaton.." I continued to look at him confused. "Was she the love of your life?" I asked to break the silence. "Was?" he shouted. "How dare you use her name in the past tense, how dare you; you ignorant fool!" he shouted, lifting up his cane. His eyes changed, they brimmed over with tears, his voice shaking. "I'm sorry sir! Is she the love of your life?" I asked, correcting myself. He put down his cane and looked down, breathing heavily. He said nothing, just continued to stare down and I sat there in silence, afraid that I was going to tick him off if I spoke again.

"Emma Veaton is the most beautiful girl i have met and had the privilege of falling in love with," he said in a soft cracked voice. "She is my everything. She is the air I breathe, this water I drink, this food I eat and this very smile I wear."

"Where is she now sir?" I asked softly. There was a brief pause, and then he looked up with moist eyes and said, "I don't know!"

CHAPTER FOUR

THE DESCRIPTION

I sat there, waiting for him to speak; but he just sat staring down into his cup and said nothing. It seemed as if time had paused, the world had stopped spinning. I was curious to find out more about this girl he spoke about, but I was still too afraid to break the silence.

"Forever in her debt I shall lie." he spoke breaking the silence.

I adjusted myself in my seat eager to listen to him speak. "This debt of love, I can never return. I realised the sacrifices she had made, but it was a little too late. Her silence always outweighed my anger, her patience, like a calm sweet winter breeze. Her love was pure, straight from the heart. Every day, over time; I fell deeper and deeper into this debt of love," he said in a soft voice.

"I still remember the first time I laid my eyes on her. A couple of us friends had decided to meet up and she happen to be a friend of a friend. She was dressed in black and white. Her hair tied into a beautiful bun and her smile, slightly curving the edges of her lips slightly downwards. She was short, barely reaching up to my chin," he said, touching his chin trying to show her height in comparison. She stood there at a distance, with a couple of her friends and one of them said something funny and she began to laugh, covering half of her face with her hands. She had barely lowered her hand, but her laughter got the better of her and she just covered her entire face, laughing. I could not hear the laughter as she was at a distance, but in my head it sounded like a choir at the church, like a million waves crashing at the shore during sunset. "The minute I saw her, I saw a home and not a hotel room and that's when I knew, she was the one. I walked up to her and introduced myself and the minute she turned to me and I looked into her eyes, my heartbeat dropped. I was in a state of wonder. I was not used to this. We usually have an adrenaline rush when we are excited due to the release of catecholamines in our body; but why was I feeling so calm with this stranger I just met. I was trying to figure out my reaction when she looked up at me and said, 'Hi, I'm Emma Veaton; you can call me EV.' She had the sweetest voice, perfect texture I would say," Dr. Fletcher said, as he continued to describe her. I noticed how he changed when he spoke about her, he had this magical glow, and his smile was beyond imagination and his entire face lit up like a thousand light bulbs. His hands moved haphazardly in all directions as he spoke. "We spent almost a good 3–4 hours that day. The group of friends I mean, even though I hadn't noticed anyone else once I started talking to her. The others were just a bundle of hay stacks," he said, laughing. I couldn't help but smile listening to this. "Before we left that day, I asked her if I could have her telephone number and she gladly obliged. I couldn't wait to run back home and ring her up. And so, I ran like the wind, completely oblivious to the streets and the people and cars honking by. Young blood in me back in those days," he said, grinning. I loved how he could just not stop smiling as he spoke of her.

I noticed that my tea had gone cold, although, I didn't care as I took a sip. "I reached home, and I remember throwing my coat on the floor, and running towards my stair case. I slipped and fell towards the end of the staircase, but I just didn't care. I got back up and ran upstairs, this time holding the railing, of course. I ran into the corner of my room where I had placed the brand new telephone that I had purchased, and I stood there in front of it. I was sweating from my warm up exercise of running you see. Sweat dripped from my forehead onto the phone. I stopped, took a couple of deep breaths and then began dialling her number, "0161 911 6050," he whispered, dialling in the air on an imaginary telephone. "Tring tring, tring tring," he cried out imitating the ringing tone. "Ha, no answer!" he shouted. There was pause, and then he continued, "My smile faded, I felt so sad. Why did she not pick up? I hung up the phone disappointed and sat on the floor. But then it hit me. Wait a minute, I ran like a gazelle being chased by a lion. She must have not yet reached home," I told myself and got up and I began to dance only to slip and fall again," he said.

My mind kept diving in, deeper and deeper into his story. I was so intrigued by his vivid descriptions of her; I could not help but be curious as to where this was going. He took a few sips of his tea and then continued, "I sat there anxiously waiting to call her again. But I didn't want to call too soon. I guess I was scared that she wouldn't pick up the second time too. So I just kept walking around in my room, thinking about her the whole time."

"After a while, don't know how long since we totally lose track of conscious time and Einstein's theory of relativity will be having its full effect on us, I gathered up the courage to pick up the telephone one more time."

"0161 911 6050!" he said, slowly, in a deep voice again, dialling on an imaginary telephone in front of him. "Tring tring, tring tring.

'Hello'

She had picked up and I could feel my heart beats give up on me and for a moment, I almost felt like I was going to fall down from all the emotions rushing within me.

Err, hi, it's me Fletcher, Aaron Fletcher, I said, with the weirdest voice ever and you know what her reply was boy?" he asked, grinning as he did. I nodded my head waiting for him to answer.

"Shit!" he exclaimed. "Shit was her first word to me over the telephone. I had imagined a thousand ways of how our first conversation would go and a million things she would speak about, but never did I think her first word to me would be that," he said, chuckling. "We had a great conversation that night over the phone and I was too lost in our conversations, that I had forgotten to ask her why she had reacted the way she did and EV as you know, just let it slip off. It was only the following day that I found out through my friends that they had placed a bet for 3 pounds with her saying that I would give her a call, the same day. When I found this out, I gave a casual reply understanding that, this assumption of me they had was much better than the entire reality of the incident; rest said and done, I was happy for my friends who, I had made 3 pounds richer through my actions of love," he said, with a wide smile.

I sat there continuing to listen to Dr. Fletcher as he spoke.

"What happened then Dr. Fletcher?" I asked unable to bear the silence breaks.

"Then? My ignorance took over, that's what happened. That's the thing about your first love. No matter how much you love them and in how many ever ways, you will mess up in more ways than you can imagine, because all the things you will do, will be your first. I was a raging young man, filled with arrogance and ego and an impulsive behaviour for which I would fall prey to more often than not," he said. I could sense a tone of regret in his voice, and his mind, clouded with memories of things he had done wrong. "Did you hurt her?" I asked, somehow gathering up the courage.

"In more ways that you can imagine!" he said in a broken voice. "It's not that I did not love her. I did, my God; I did with all my heart, soul and fire within. I loved her so much that I, an atheist began to pray for her. Just her, nothing for me, I was willing to make every single disbelief into a belief, anything for EV. Maybe I loved her too much," he said with tears rolling down his face and voice all cracked up. I poured a glass of water and handed it to him.

"Argh, more sympathy. Here drink it yourself, fool.," he shouted, handing me the glass of water. "drink it I said, you fool," he shouted again. "That's all right, I don't want it sir," I replied, with a soft voice, no longer scared of his temper as I had gotten the hang of the kind of person he is. "What did you say? Say it again, I couldn't hear you.," he shouted. "I'm fine without the water sir," I replied, louder and clearer this time. "Exactly, that's what we do boy! When we are offered things we don't need, we refuse it. I don't need your sympathy. Give it to those who ask for it, who crave it. Not to a person like me, to men who are in love. We don't need it."

It was at this moment I realised his passion. It was pure. I also realised that he may have regretted certain actions of his, but not his love for her.

"Let us continue to rebel. Against love and against hate. Against wars and against peace. Against compromises and against solitude," he began speaking, closing his eyes and opening it midway and staring down angrily at me for some reason. "Write it down you fool, lest you want to forget. Write it down.," he shouted. I quickly ran to the counter and grabbed a pen and a piece of paper and began writing down as he spoke, which to my astonishment, he began reciting before I could even reach back to the table. I must have missed a couple of sentences. By the time he had stopped reciting, this I was holding in my hands.

Let us continue to rebel
Against love and against hate
Against wars and against peace
Against compromises and against solitude
Let us continue to rebel
Against emotions we feel
And against the emotions we make others feel
Let us continue to rebel
Until finally, one day
We become rebellious against rebels.
Let us continue to rebel.

I had another look at these words and then I looked up at him and there he was back to staring out of the window, taking in deep breaths which I figured, was in an attempt to catch the fragrance.

I think that's the thing about us humans, we are such wonderful creatures; that when we are actually moved by stories and people, we can't help but fall into their stories completely and fall in love with them.

"These are wonderful words sir," I said to him. He said nothing, just continued to stare out and trace the raindrops as they rolled down the window.

"What happened then sir?" I asked clearly realising by now that I didn't like even a moment of silence.

"Then she left me, boy!" he said, in a firm voice and now there was a silence which even I could not break.

CHAPTER FIVE

THE DEPARTURE: JANUARY 6TH

"She left not for another," he spoke, finally breaking the silence. "She left, not because I was hurting her, she left because she felt she was hurting me. Over the years, we really got to know each other. I had shared with her all that I held close to my heart and over a period of time, somehow she had become a part of me. She was asking me to let go of her, not realising that in the process I'd have to let go of a piece of myself. I remember completely breaking down, falling to her feet holding her by her shoes begging her not to leave. I told her time and again that she was not hurting me and not for a second ever did she ever make me feel unwanted. I looked at her and there was not a single tear in her eyes and here I was completely drenched in my own.," he said, beginning to cry, again. This time though, I was not stupid enough to offer him water.

"When you know a person to such an extent of rawness, time becomes insignificant. You stop assessing the depth of your bond with them by time, instead by the fact that, at the time of trouble, or when you are hurt, it is to them that you first reach out to. Even when they are not there for you,

you forgive them because in your head you have already created a perfect version of them, the one who could never be wrong in any context, whatsoever"

"Over time, I think I just lost sight of what brought us to this exact moment," he added. "For the most of it, I think it was the fact that I loved her too much and she very well knew it, and she could see what I had for her was real. But with whatever reasons she had, she did not share the same set of emotions for me or maybe, she did in her own way and somehow, that made her believe that she was a dreadful bond which I was just not willing to sever. Knowing Emma, she was strong enough to do it for me," he added, wiping his tears.

"She did love me; that I know for sure. If a human heart beats for an average of 72 beats per minute, I am sure that at least 10 of them were for me and that was enough for me. But she continued to explain to an ignorant idiot like me to not settle for just 10 while there are people out there, who probably would have 72 beats in my name."

His words were interrupted by sudden coughing by the person sitting behind him. It was an old lady, and I remember asking the lady to shut up in my head. I guess, I just did not want any interruptions.

"Finally, I gathered myself together and pulled myself up," he continued, once the lady was done with her coughing.

"I got up, and I remember looking at my watch and it was 2:45 PM, on the 6th of January. I told her to take her time. I told her that she was going to get a year without me in her life. A complete absence of Aaron Fletcher. She would not hear from me, she would not see me; she would not hear how I was faring from my friends, a year without my existence in her life. I remember, she tried to stop me in between, telling me that it was a stupid idea because she knew me too well and knowing my history of going on and off with her, she clearly knew this was a terrible idea. But by now, my sadness and tears had turned to frustration and anger," Dr. Fletcher said and I could sense the change in his voice and tone as he spoke.

"One year from now, on the 6th of January, at 2:45 PM exact, you will give me a call and you will tell me if you want me in your life or you don't. I remember, she tried to convince me right then that she did want me in her life but for some weird reason I refused to understand," he said with a disgusted face.

"I remember punching the side wall out of frustration, that she could not discrete my feelings for her". "In one year, you will make that phone call and irrespective of what your answer is, you will call me up and you will tell me. Figure out what I am to you and then tell me. I don't care what the answer is, but that phone call must happen. If it is a 'yes,' then we know we both want the same thing, and if it is a 'no' and I don't give a damn about the reason, I will let you go."

Dr. Fletcher by now was firm in his words, staring hard into space, almost as if he was speaking to an Emma who was right in front of him.

"I Remember punching the wall again in anger, as I walked out so that my mind would divert to the pain on my broken knuckles and my agony would ablate and I remember shouting as I walked out, 'That call is a must' and I did not even turn around to look at her," he said, showing the little finger of his left hand which was slightly crooked.

"Did it hurt sir?" I asked. "Of course it did, you fool! Do u know how delicate these fingers of mine are?" he shouted. "Not your fingers sir. You, did it hurt you?" I corrected myself. "Ah, I wouldn't say hurt; but yes, I did feel something as I walked away. It's like you take anger, frustration, sadness and a little pinch of sugar and you blend it well. These are all primitive emotions, boy. Feeling these things are common and almost all of us do so at some point of time or the other; but the mixture it takes to make the blend is the thing which makes the difference.

"If I may ask Dr. Fletcher, why did you say one year to be exact?" I asked him. "Isn't it simple my boy? It's because we all crave for dramatic endings, don't we!" he replied laughing. "I guess you are right sir," I replied, realising what he said was true. No matter how realistic we try to keep our lives, we do think of a lot of dramatic circumstances in our heads, the beauty of a human brain. "Ha! I know I am right!" he exclaimed. "But to be honest my boy, one year is not a small period of time. When the matter at hand is love, a day seems like a year. They say life is too short, but when it is a life either of wait, or of regret, life is too long," he said in a soft voice. "Do you regret loving her sir?" I asked. "No, no, no, no!" he exclaimed, moving both his hands vigorously knocking both the glasses off the table. "Love is like a seed. It needs a little bit of sunshine, a little bit of rain. It needs nurturing, it needs patience. And when it finally blooms, recognise it for what it is and not for what it could have been. You can sow it deeper into the soil, water it more than required, and shine out a thousand rays of light. But it will grow and bloom only when it's time comes. Just take in a deep breath and take in the fragrance of the flowers.," he said, taking in deep breaths with his eyes closed. "Taste the wonderful fruits of life, and rest under its shadow when you exhaust yourself. Watch how the seed of love grows and supports you in this battle against the world with strength and courage and you shall be set free of all your fears."

Music, his words were pure music to my ears. It had been so long that I heard something so powerful and that's when the waitress came up to me and said, "You'll be charged extra for those," pointing at the broken glasses. I obliged as at the point in time, I didn't care for anything else. The thunder soon began to rumble and I realised that I had forgotten my umbrella yet again and I did not want to get drenched in the rain again as my body could already sense an inevitable cold from my previous experience. "I'd better be on my way now sir. I do not want to get drenched," I told him. "Are you here for a while?" I asked him, as I put on my coat. "Yes, I am," he replied. I bid him goodbye and as I was walking out, I looked at him once again and there he was, back to scribbling in his book.

CHAPTER SIX

AFTERTHOUGHT

Back home, I lay in my bed, all covered up in my comforter, yet another sleepless night. But this time though, it was because of Dr. Fletcher and his words. I had found a weird sense of respect for him. I could sense the passion in his words. I used to believe that words are always just mere words. I still do stand by them, but after listening to the man speak, I was beginning to feel that words too could carry a level of depth if they were either preceded by or followed by actions irrespective of after how long they take to happen. I began to feel restless. I kicked away my comforter with my legs and sat back up. As the second hand ticks on the clock, my mind ticked with Rachel's name. 'Why this ego?' I asked myself. I still remember her words from the last time we spoke, "Why are you doing this to me Sam? Why are you pushing me away?" she said, right here outside my door. "I am not pushing you away Rachel, I'm not doing anything. You are the one who is doing it all," I replied.

"How do expect me to be okay with this Sammy? Listen to your heart closely and for once think of us and think of all the memories of our days together. Once you do that, you will realise that all the things I know about you is because I asked you about them and all the things you know about me, is because I told you about them. Do you not see how sad this is?" she asked, her voice beginning to break.

"I do. I guess I fucked up. Initially I fell in love with you because I was tired of being hurt by the loss of people in my life and you were always there for me and you became a priority and in time my darling, I began loving you in so many ways that now I think I love you so much that I don't think I will be able to go days without you. The ironic part is, I was so scared of being alone and in that process, I fell in love with you and I'm afraid that if I get any closer to you than I already have, I won't have the strength to survive your loss," I replied again, with that annoying helpless smile of mine, which even I had begun to get annoyed with but for some reason, could never help wearing it.

"Take a chance, take this chance. You love me, I love you and that's more than what most people get in a life time Sammy. What makes you think I'll leave you one day?" she said to me, her eyes again beginning to moisten and every time I saw that, a part of me would die inside because every time, it was me on the other end responsible for those tears and it killed me. I realised very early on that there is no one else more perfect for me than Rachel, and maybe that's why my words and emotions came out in such a tangled mess.

"Everybody leaves Rach, everybody does. Either by choice or by force or just out of pure fucked up fate," I said, still unable to wipe that weird helpless smile off my face and that pitiful voice. Yet again, she turned around in frustrated and ran crying. I stood there by the door, watching her run into the rain, getting drenched in the rain and I could hear my heart shout out to me, 'Go after her, you moron. Don't let her fade away into the rain, go after her,' but, like in every emotional situation I've been in, my legs had left my body and were no longer under my motor command.

I shook myself out of this flashback and got up from my bed and went to my study, and sat there staring into a blank piece of paper and decided to write down what I was feeling at the moment. I had this habit that I would follow wherein, when my mind was in a confused state, I would just sit and write down anything and everything that came to my mind and would do so with absolutely no filter whatsoever. It had been a while since I had done this, so I gave it a shot and began to write with no mental inhibition whatsoever.

Ever wonder, why silence leads to the loudest of the thoughts?

Ever wonder, why you fear the dark, while in reality, it's the brightest of the memories that haunt us the most.

Ever wonder, how a fragrance from the past, overpowers the roses of the present?

Ever wonder how at times you find God in someone else but you fail to find faith in yourself?

Ever wonder, how in this rapidly changing world, you find yourself unchanged at times?

Ever wonder, why negativity sticks within and refuses to let go whereas positivity always find a way to escape out?

Tell me, do you ever wonder?

I took a breath and read what I had written and felt so pathetic by the end of it. 'You idiot' I told myself. I still was the same frightened fool. I tore the paper into pieces and went back to bed.

CHAPTER SEVEN

AFTERLIFE

The next day, I went to the cafeteria with a book in hand, hoping to take down some of his words. He was right there where he always was, the same spot. It was almost as if he had not moved. The only difference was his clothes, and his hair seemed to have been combed for the first time since I had met him. I grabbed my tea from the counter and walked up to his table.

"Looking all smart today Dr. Fletcher," I told, greeting him. He just smiled. "It seems like it's almost the 16th of July, doesn't it?", he said, with a smile. "Almost sir, just 2 days to go," I replied with a smile.

"Ah yes, I knew it, her fragrance is getting stronger isn't it?," he asked. "Yes sir, it is. Believe it or not sir, Emma's essence is irreplaceable and unmistakable," I was not lying to him, I truly had begun to experience this powerful lady that he had talked of. I too, could not help but begin to experience her. The cafeteria seemed slightly brighter, people seemed happier than they did yesterday. The food and tea seemed to taste better too.

"The sun seems brighter today doesn't she?" Dr. Fletcher told looking out the window. "She sure is", I replied, looking out the window.

"She was my sunshine," he uttered. "Bright and radiant, filled with fire. More often than not, the sun is referred to as a 'he' and the moon as a 'she.' It's because of the assumption that the sun is red, powerful and filled with fire and this ignorant world we live in wrongly compares it to a man. Fools! The minute I looked at her, I realised that if the sun is anything, she's a lady like EV; filled with warmth; bright and radiant, spreading life and light; and me, like the moon, shining from the light she gives me. If today, you see anything beautiful in me, it is because of her, selfless enough to let me claim the sacred night as my own."

I sat there and for the first time in years, I felt my eyes moistening. 'Who is this man?' I asked myself. More importantly, who was she? Was she really so wonderful to bring such a man to his knees in every way? I had new questions popping up in my head. His descriptions of her feel were so surreal that I was slowly, helplessly beginning to fall in love with Emma Veaton.

"The minute we departed, my heart was still within my chest, but the beats, I had left them in her hands," Dr. Fletcher said.

"I see you boy, a stranger to me and you might think of me as a mad man for talking to you about such random things, but I do not care!" he shouted. "I do not care for you, for that lady at the counter and nor do I care for all the people who asked me to move on" he continued shouting. I gently held his hand in both of mine and told him in a calm voice, "I do not think of you as a mad man, nor a stranger, sir." I could see it in his face that my words had calmed him down. "I spent months, months waiting for her phone call. I knew very well that just hoping for the day to come sooner, would not make it come any sooner than it would. I remember taking a taxi everyday back home at 2 and stare at my telephone for an hour." I kept writing down everything he spoke.

By now, there were tears in my eyes, but I quickly wiped them off to make sure that he would not see them. I did not want to him get the idea that I was feeling sorry for him.

"12 C,
61 Wellfield road,
Roth,
Manchester," he shouted.
"12 C,
61 Wellfield road,
Roth,
Manchester," he shouted again, waving his hands out. I figured he was picturing himself grabbing the taxi. An odd way of shouting out the address and stopping the taxi, I thought to myself.

"I remember, storming into the house, throwing my coat by the hanger, taking a right as swiftly as I could and running upstairs and running into my room which was straight down the hallway bursting open the door and staring at my telephone which was in the corner of the room. My telephone lay brightly lit in the corner with light. The light from my window opposite was obstructed by huge branches from a tree outside and the light would fall perfectly, only on half of the wall, the side which had the telephone. Bless that tree!" he exclaimed. I couldn't help but smile. His descriptions made me realise how we tend to assign values to irrelevant things and soon it gains such a value that it becomes priceless. He could have chosen to not observe the pattern of the sunlight at all and chose to ignore that tree. Men do funny things when in love. I understood it so well because I could think of at least ten such things I did with Rachel, and she on the other hand, completely oblivious to those actions. But that's the beauty of such actions, I believe. If they are explained or if they are shown to the significant other, they lose all its value. The fact that he was an atheist, but he chose to pray for her speaks volumes of his passion for her. The way, he assigned value to things because he attached a piece of her into all the immaterial things, soon they had a life of their own. He knew that she would call him only on the 6thof January of the coming year and yet he would wait everyday by the phone. This was what love was all about.

"I would look eagerly at my watch, and when it struck 2:44, I would close my eyes and pray, hoping that today she would have realised how much she really loves me and would give me a call. As I closed my eyes every day by the phone, I realised that seconds turned into minutes and I confirmed two things. Time flies when I think about her and also, my chest would hurt every time I opened my eyes, only to find that the time was past 3PM."

He took a pause. I could sense he was emotionally drained. I assumed the flashbacks were too powerful for him to handle. He began gulping down his glass of water. He refilled the glass and gulped it down completely almost choking on it and spitting out some water. I didn't move a muscle as by now, I had completely figured out the kind of man Dr. Fletcher was and could sense actions that would tick him off.

He wiped himself and then continued to speak, "I often wonder how I broke, like the clouds giving way to the sunlight. Wondering to myself if these were the same clouds that struck down lightnings with all their fury, and I told myself, that she really was the only sunshine who had the light strong enough to break through my thunderous clouds."

I sensed that he was indicating that he had a troubled past and EV somehow made it better for him or perhaps helped him through it and maybe that's why he fell for her in words beyond explanation.

"Listen boy," he said, trying to clear the hoarseness in his voice by coughing. "I want to be left alone for a while; could you give me some space?"

"Of course Dr. Fletcher," I replied. I got up and left without another word. I had realised that, he was emotionally drained. As I walked out, I caught a glimpse of him like I always did, but this time he just sat there. He didn't write, but sat there hanging his head.

CHAPTER EIGHT

THE FRAGRANCE OF LOVE

I met this girl; her hair was like the night sky
I met this girl, her eyes were like the night sky
Her smile, as innocent as a child
And that soul, as pure as the winter snow
I ask myself; who is she?
She came into my life like a cold sea breeze
Filling my heart and soul with peace
She turns all my darkness into light
And all my sadness into joy
I ask myself; who is she?
She makes my days all bright
I walk with this faint smile
She erases all my fears
And now I know for sure,
She's an angel with a smile.

Tears began to roll down my face, as I read this along with many other poems I had written for Rachel. I had never given her a single one of them. I kept them all stacked up in a pile. As I read these poems at home, my emotions came running back to me, the rush of blood I felt that made my body go warm every time I hugged her. The time I lost myself in oblivion the first time my lips touched hers. I sat there, asking myself, 'Why am I this afraid?' I literally saw no one other than Rachel in front of me, or in my dreams. I sat there wondering. Am I a fool or am I a coward? Am I a fool to push her away even though she meant the world to me? Or am I just a coward who is too scared to get close to another person. Maybe I'm still hurting from my past I told myself. Maybe I am not a fool, or a coward for that matter. Maybe my fear of pain was too potent for me to overcome and even a person as good as Rachel was not good enough for me to overcome them. Or perhaps she was so good that, my fear of losing her in a way of no return overcame my love for her. I began to lose control of my mind. I was dying to give her a call. I walked up to my telephone; I stood there staring at it. I could already hear Rachel's voice in my head. It sounded so beautiful. I pictured that perfect smile of hers which she would have when she heard my voice. But then, my fears were too strong for me to overcome and I turned and walked away.

The ghosts from our chained past, often kill the free spirits of the future!

Why was love so complicated? The emotion in itself is so simple, but when the matter at hand comes to expression, it comes out in ways you can never think of and it progresses in directions we could never think of due to various catalysts such an anger, ego and selfishness acting on it.

I sat there listening to some wonderful music and I realised that I had begun to feel comfortable in this mess. Anything I guess, when kept static for too long, ultimately grows on you; good or bad!

Such a simple elegant emotion love is, but complicated by so many layers. Those who are bound by it are bound forever. It completes you and it can also destroy you.

Here I was, feeling that this love was killing me softly, on the other hand, there was Dr. Fletcher who was at the other end of the pole. He was everything I was not and maybe perhaps that's why I was drawn to him. His words were perhaps what I needed, the perspective I could never have. But his words, although had an emotional impact on me, did not seem to bring about changes in my actions. Perhaps in the end, words are just mere words!

It's funny how I almost felt like I was living two lives, two completely different love stories. The sad part was that I was falling deeper and deeper into the story of Dr. Fletcher while all I could do with my own was just contemplate my decisions remain indolent. My respect for the old man continued to grow. But of what use is inspiration of any sort if we don't implement them in our actions. We seek inspiration every day, especially from another person. We convince ourselves by saying that, 'If they could do it, so can we.' But why do we just leave it at that? Why is it so hard for us to take action, to initiate the first step? Here I was listening to probably one of the greatest stories I had heard and all I could do was listen and wonder as to how a person in love does what he does. It was questions like these that made me think if I even loved Rachel at times.

Why is that, I was able to believe in his story so passionately but lacked the same passion in mine?

I felt like I was converting Rachel into a black hole, the darkest thing known to exist. Not even light can escape a black hole. The irony is that a black hole is nothing but a dead star which radiated light for years and then finally collapsed. Does she even deserve pain like this, that too from an incompetent moron like me?

Dr. Fletcher seemed much better and happier and at peace than yesterday, when I looked at him. He had his wonderful smile back, his eyes were sparkling.

"How are you feeling today, Dr. Fletcher?" I asked. "I feel like I am beginning to fall in love all over again boy. I feel her fragrance right around the corner," he replied.

I loved how he related to her fragrance as a feel and not a smell. That's what real beauty is all about, isn't it? When we look at a beautiful flower from afar, we are stunned by its beauty and we continue to admire it. But as we get closer, we begin to feel its fragrance and it's so beautiful that we can't help but close our eyes completely giving in to its fragrance.

"How does she make you feel sir?" I asked. "Like lying down on a bed made of a thousand lilies," he replied smiling, swaying his body to some imaginary music that was playing in his head.

"I change the lilies in my jar, next to the telephone every day for my beloved sunshine," he said. "Her warmth keeps the Lilly's fresh. I've got to buy a whole bunch soon, I feel like July 16th is right here around the corner," he added.

"It's tomorrow sir," I replied, showing him the date on my watch.

He looked at it closely and then said, "I had a watch very similar to this one. I had such a wonderful relationship with that watch. It got me closer to Emma every day. I loved how it kept moving forward every day and the dates kept changing and the time marching on closer and closer to her phone call."

"Sir, was she not supposed to call on you the 6th of January?" I asked, confused. "Yes, yes my boy! You are right. The 6th of January, that's what we had decided on, the 6th of January, you are absolutely right," he replied.

"Sir, if I may ask, then why are you so keen on the 16th of July?" I asked him.

He looked at me and began to smile and then closed his eyes and took a deep breath.

"July 16th is the day that I first met Emma, my boy!" he exclaimed.

CHAPTER NINE

JULY THE 16TH

"My day on the 16th of July started out just as any other day for me, completely distasteful. I hated how bright the sun was, I was missing my clouds and my rain which synchronised with my mood. My only motivation to get up from my bed was my friend who had said that today I would finally get to meet this girl called Emma who he had just gotten to know."

Dr. Fletcher began to narrate the day and I sat all ears, listening to every word he uttered, writing them down.

He continued to narrate, not stopping even for a second and I continued to write down every detail.

"Over the past few days, my friend had spent lots of time with her and he could not stop talking about how comfortable it was hanging out with her. I was intrigued right back then, as we always relate beauty to a face, but I just could not seem to picture her for some reason. I began to picture a comfortable, laughing, happier me talking to her based on how my friend had described her. It was weird for some reason." he said.

I could sense the excitement in his voice as he spoke. There was also a tinge of nervousness for sure.

"I was so excited that I remember thanking my friend for finally making us meet. She obviously had no idea, but I on the other hand, could not stop asking about her every day. I guess, I was craving for a change in my life and somehow I imagined her to be the change." Dr. Fletcher said, scratching his head as he laughed.

"I remember looking at my watch, time and again waiting for it to strike 4 as we had all decided to meet then. Of course I had reached a good thirty minutes early and obviously, they reached only by 4:30. That one hour, I had the most anxious moments of my life, as I sat there wondering if they would show up. I remember combing my hair every five minutes and rubbing my hands against each other harder and harder every once in a while. For some reason, it kept getting colder." he said, as he began to rub his hands vigorously. I guess, the nervousness started coming back to him and he could not help but start feeling cold.

"Then it finally happened!" he exclaimed. "They entered, and I remember vividly, my head going down after I first got a glimpse of her. My face felt like it was going to tear from the smile I was wearing. I could not look at her for more than five seconds without looking down. The minute she laughed, it was like the sound of a thousand rain drops gently falling down to earth."

There was such excitement in his voice as he spoke, I could not help but begin to feel happy and I too started to smile.

"By the end of the day, I remember all of the members were scattered across the room, talking, playing and I remember taking a seat to have a bite and she stood there across the room. As I ate, I noticed that she began to walk towards to me and then, she sat down next to me. My head began to feel dizzy, I remember my eyes went all blurry and I looked at her and smiled and she said, 'I like your eyes, I see something in them.' That's it! I was done for! I didn't care if it was the first time we met, I didn't care if she was already seeing someone, which she was not, I didn't care for anything and I was in doubt of everything but one thing I knew for sure, that I was in love with Emma Veaton!," he exclaimed, laughing with happiness.

I stopped writing and closed my book and I just looked at him. I began to wonder, how he could place her on such a high pedestal. Such perfection in a human being, how was it possible? Was she some kind of divine intervention who entered his life to save him from his misery? Listening to the way he described her, I thought to myself that she must have been an extra-terrestrial of some sort. I lost my attention off his speech, for the first time, not because I was bored. I just sat there looking at him describing her and listening to it, made me realise one thing. A person lives a million love stories with another person in their heart and minds. I thought to myself, this whole incident that he had explained, would have been just mere hours to Emma because she was unaware of the things going on in his head, the things he had undergone mentally and emotionally. When in love, the mental effort a person puts in goes unnoticed and the action itself comes out small or more often than not, unworthy of notice. Maybe that's why we find love to be so powerful. We emotionally attach ourselves and every action of ours is with the other person in mind either voluntarily, or involuntarily. I had lost Dr. Fletcher for the first time as he continued to speak of the 16th of July, but I could not help but try to understand the magnitude of his love. I didn't know if they were actually together, if Emma even loved him, nor did I know the reason as to why he was in the place that he was in right now. I started to feel a sense of fear of some sort, as he continued to describe her, and I was afraid that my emotions were soon going to manifest on my face and so I just excused myself and ran out. I remember, running so fast, to get away from his words, as now they had begun to make me question my love for Rachel. My situation seemed like a small creeper crawling its way up his massive story, trying to gain some kind of inspiration from him. But now, I started to feel scared. Scared, because I established that his love story was the greatest one I had ever heard irrespective of what the reality of it was and I told myself that I was no Aaron Fletcher to make it work. I was terrified and I remember running like the wind, but I was unable to get away from his words. I ran back home and shut the door behind me.

Finally, there was silence again and my heartbeat was the only thing I could hear as I sat there in silence surrounded by darkness.

CHAPTER TEN

UNPOSTED LOVE LETTERS

I went back to the poems I had written to Rachel and started to notice how the contents of my poems had changed over time.

> *I still remember that night*
> *She was all in smiles*
> *The stars filled the sky*
> *And love filled our hearts*
> *Happiness was here*
> *Surrounding us for real*
> *I looked into her eyes*
> *And asked her what love is?*
> *She replied with a smile*
> *Love is sacrifice!*

I remember I had written this down after we had spent a night at her place, star gazing from her balcony and she had shared some of her stories of the past from which I had truly understood the kind of person Rachel was and how she would go to any lengths to keep another person happy, even at the cost of her own. It was the first time, I felt like I was in love with her. But obviously, I did not have the courage to tell her that back then nor could I express myself and tell her how strong I thought she really was.

Reading this poem brought a smile to my face and I kept it aside. I, then, continued to read the next one.

She says she loves a melody
Little does she know, she's no less than a symphony
She dances like there is no tomorrow
Making my today, a brighter day
She flies without her wings
Reaching for the stars
Redefining hope
A hope to live, a hope to love, a hope to laugh
She narrates her stories, with a smile
Captivating my heart
I reply with a smile,
Hoping that she would read my eyes
Telling her she redefines my hope,
A hope to live, a hope to love, a hope to laugh.

As I read these lines, tears filled my eyes. I had written this probably somewhere after 2 years of being with her. How was it that I had failed to express these emotions to her, even though I felt them so strongly? Why is it that we feel one way but we portray another emotion, by the end of which, even we are left to wonder as to why we did the things we did and said the words we didn't mean? Here I was, in one extreme struggle to express my emotions and show my true self to Rachel and in the other end, was Dr. Fletcher, who expressed every single bit of his emotion with such depth and clarity even though, Emma was no longer there in his life. He had, not an inch of regret or a pinch of hatred. His words still echo in my heart when I had asked him if somewhere in the corner of his heart he had hated Emma.

"If there's even an inch of hatred for Emma in my body, when I die, and I am buried with that hatred within me, the mud of this earth shall refuse to stick to my casket," he said.

What was this love? I felt like it was too small a word to even describe what he had for Emma. Here I was, struggling to face my own emotions.

I remembered then, that tomorrow was the 16th of July and so I thought, I'd make the day a little more special for him by writing a letter to him. I wanted to let him know how inspirational he and his story had been in my life.

I sat in my study, and began to write the letter, and this time, with purposeful intention of giving it to the other person, unlike my previous self, who would have probably just added it to the pile of the other undelivered letters.

Dear Dr. Fletcher

I write to you, not with an intention of praise. I write to you today, only to express my respect for you. We all love to hear great stories, but through you, I got to truly live one. You helped me realise that love is not a theorem you prove. It is not a fact. It is neither created nor shall it ever cease to exist. It's the warmth of the sunshine shining on our faces. It's the moistness of the tears rolling down our face, and you helped me realise that we are all time travellers in our lives, with love as the vessel that carries us all. I stay confused as to whether I love the lady of my life enough to let her any closer to this flame that I am living in, and I have fears in me which inhibit me from getting close to her and keep me away from her. Listening to you, helps me get a better perspective. I hope to finally overcome my fears one day and let her in closer and am sure that I can give her more happiness than pain. Till that day comes, I shall keep your words close and I shall continue to stay inspired by your story.

Thank you for everything Dr. Fletcher.

Love,
Sam Gray

I folded the letter and kept it in my coat to ensure that Id not forget it the next day. I knew for sure I wouldn't, but I guess I just didn't want to take the chance. I went to bed that night oddly satisfied with myself, amongst all the mess that I had created for myself.

CHAPTER ELEVEN

THE STAND UP

My walk to Jimmie's the next day was filled with excitement and curiosity. It was finally the 16th of July and I too could not help but feel excited for it. Somehow, I had gotten completely captivated by all of this. My mind, continued to imagine and picture a happy Dr. Fletcher enjoying the Emma all around him. I thought of asking him today, what had happened on the day of the phone call which he was supposed to receive on the 6th of January and where Emma was at the moment. No matter how happy I was for him, I had to find out what actually happened on the day of the phone call and find out what Emma's reply was.

How could such a wonderful love story come to be where it was right now? From all the conversations I had with him so far, I truly understood the essence of a love story. I did not know Emma at all, but I had nothing but respect and love for her. My only image of her was from the way he described her and she was nothing short of beautiful.

But first things first, I had to give him my letter. To be honest, I was a bit anxious. I was taking an emotional step forward.

I walked up to him and there he was at the same chair, smiling to himself and writing down in his book like he always does.

"Good evening Dr. Fletcher, how are you today?" I asked, as I sat down. "I am excellent my dear stranger boy!" he exclaimed.

I could see how happy he was and I guess that's the thing about happiness; it shows no matter how hard you try to hide it.

"I have something for you," I said, in a soft voice as I handed him the letter I had written the previous night.

"Oh, a letter, I love letters!" he replied, curiously unfolding it. He began reading the letter and I could not help but smile, because I felt I had taken an emotional step forward by trying to express myself in the vague way I did, but I was proud, as it was raw, unfiltered. I sat there; looking at him read the letter. He looked at me for a second and shrugged his shoulders and then continued to read the letter. His smile had faded away and then, out of the blue, he tore the letter to a million pieces and threw it against the window.

I was shocked! I was unable to digest what I was seeing and I was trying to figure out what had just happened.

"Coward!" he exclaimed. "You don't deserve her love. You don't love her. If you did, you would not be in doubt. Ignorant fools around me. All of you! I am no inspiration to anyone. I don't intend to change the world with my story, it's my story, and it's mine! I don't need your opinions of me or Emma. How dare you talk to me? How dare you give me this letter? All of you are the same; all of you wish that if your situation was different, your stories would be different. You guys fail to take initiative and have a million useless excuses to back up your cowardice. You people are sad versions of human beings. You disgust me!" he shouted.

"But I do love her. The very reason it's killing me softly is because I love her so much!" I replied trying to hold on to my breaking voice.

"You don't love her! You may be a stranger to me, but your words don't deceive me. You coward! Love does not kill, it keeps you alive! You don't love her!" he shouted, his voice getting louder.

I didn't love her? I didn't love her? Who was this man to establish that I did not love her? I could feel my blood beginning to rush to my head. I began to tremble in anger. He continued to shout and he continued to say that I did not love her.

"Shut up!" I shouted back, I had had enough. "Shut up! You don't know the things I've been through. You haven't lived my life. You don't know how much I love her!" I shouted.

I didn't stop there; I continued to shout back having completely lost control of myself.

"You are just a sad old man who has failed in life. You sit here all alone and you tell me that I don't love her. Well if you loved Emma so much, where is she? Tell me, where the hell is the love of your life? Where is EV?" I shouted.

"How dare you?" he shouted, getting up from his chair, grabbing his cane and raising it in the air.

I took a step back, not because I was afraid. I guess deep down, I still had that respect for him irrespective of what my words were saying at the moment.

"Get out of my sight, you fool!," he shouted. "Gladly," I replied, as I walked out of the cafeteria not looking back at him to take notice of him for the first time as I exited the cafeteria.

I didn't love Rachel! How could he say that? My love for her was so pure and unconditioned. I loved her so much that it hurt.

I went back home and this time, there was no silence. My head was bursting with his voice. How could he say such a thing! How could he, of all people say that I didn't love her? How could he say all that, just by reading a letter of mine. Why did he say that? I began to get frustrated and I just started to tear out pages from any book that I found. I began to break anything that I found to be fragile in sight.

My chaotic behaviour was put to a pause from the sudden ringing of my telephone. "Rachel!" I shouted, for some reason thinking to myself that it had to be her. I ran towards the phone and picked up!

"Hello!" I shouted out loud.

"She's left us son! Your grandmother is no more! She's left us!" a sobbing voice said from the other side.

It was my dad! My grandmother was no more.

I remember that same feeling rushing back in my veins when I had lost my granddad, my knees began to shake and I fell to the floor. It began to hurt so bad inside of me.

My mother, granddad, Dr. Fletcher, Rachel and now my grandmother. I had lost yet another piece of me. My most awaited and exciting day had just turned into my worst day. It was like a nightmare that I was just unable to wake up from and it kept getting worse by the minute.

CHAPTER TWELVE

AFTERMATH

"Another round?" a voice spoke. I looked up and saw the bartender looking at me. "Yes!" I exclaimed, finishing off the remaining whiskey in my glass. I guess I found my way into one of the pubs that night. It's funny how when you're drunk, the world around you seems to revolve round and round, but your mind is fixed on just one topic! I sat there, surrounding myself in my own mess. My love for Rachel was something I had questioned a million times over. Why was I so offended when Dr. Fletcher told me that I did not love her, when I have caught myself countless times taking the road of contemplation. I sat there massaging my forehead, but the pain did not seem to show any sign of reducing. I guess the pain was not in my head. Why had I reacted that way? Why was I so offended by his words? I threw such hurtful words at him which I didn't mean at all. Why do we react in such a way? Why do we show a complete opposite emotion than the one we feel? Why do we become so impulsive? I seemed to find no starting point from where I could start to fix my crumbling life. I no longer knew what I should mourn for. Do I mourn for the loss of my grandmother or for Rachel? Do I try to fix my relationship with Dr. Fletcher by facing him or do I try to fix my past by facing them? Emotional turmoil can be such a giant baggage to carry!

"I love her!" I screamed out. But there was no one around to listen to me. I looked across and saw the bartender on the other side of the bar. "I love Rachel! I love her!" I shouted, pointing at him.

He couldn't care less, why would he? It's funny how when we are vulnerable, we try to justify everything to everyone irrespective of what we are feeling and irrespective of who we are talking to! Here I was trying to explain my unconditioned love to the bartender who didn't give a damn about the topic and somehow, I found that offensive too and I got up and left.

It was raining to the point of almost minimal vision, or perhaps it was the alcohol coursing through my blood. I took swaying steps towards my home, if I could call it that. My knees were giving up, I couldn't walk anymore. I fell flat on the footpath. "Rachel!" I shouted into the footpath, hoping that when I looked up, she would be there to pick me up. All I saw was a bunch of shoes and heels walking past me. She was not here. "Rachel!" I shouted again, louder this time with tears rolling down, which surprisingly hurt much more than they usually do and even the alcohol could not numb this pain. I pulled myself up and began to run, my vision got clearer, every time I thought of her name. I ran, my speed increased, I could see my house, I ran, faster and faster. I pushed open my door, threw my coat on the floor and ran to my telephone. I picked up the telephone and began dialling her number.

'Ring ring. Ring ring.' My body was still swaying and I stood there waiting for her to pick up. It seemed like it was ringing forever with no answer, endless, just like my life.

"Hello," finally a voice said from the other side. It was Rachel's voice.

"Hello?" the voice from the other side repeated itself.

My vocal cords had once again given up on me. I could not seem to think of even a word that I could say or maybe I had too many things to say which no words could say. I stood there, paralyzed and then I started to regain my focus. I could feel my sense coming back to me in waves and then it finally hit me. I had a moment of self-realisation. It was the sharpest thought I had. I hung up the phone.

Did I need alcohol, pain, regret and loss to realise that I loved Rachel? I was going to make one of the biggest decisions of my life and I was going to do it drunk and hurting! No ways!

It's easy to realise you need someone when you're alone, when you are hurting and vulnerable. But what happens when the vulnerability and loneliness is gone and then you realise you don't really love them and that you just needed someone. That's not love, that's selfishness. I had just realised why Dr. Fletcher said the things he did. My respect for him, soared higher up. He saw through me in just a single letter while I was finding myself to be an opaque prism giving out multiple confusing colours.

I was certain of quite a few things that night. I was definitely in love with Rachel, and I was going to fight for her and get her back into my life, but not because I needed her. Just due to the simple fact, that she completed me in ways I could have never imagined and that my life was always better and happier with her in it. I was going to get her back in my life, but with a sober mind and a clear heart. Not like this, not in this mess.

I also decided that I was going to man up and face Dr. Fletcher the next day and apologise for my actions. I was going to look him in the eye and take responsibility for my actions and apologise for all the things I had said which I did not mean. Not by letters this time, but by talking to him. I guess, I used to write letters and poems all this while because I was too afraid to tell the person what I felt and more often than not, I could not find the words. Maybe I was hiding behind the hidden, unsent letters, being a coward and convincing myself that, I was an unconditional lover, claiming that most of the things in love are best left unsaid.

The next day, before I left home, I had a good look at myself in the mirror and I saw a prouder me. I respected myself a little more. I was wearing a smile even though somewhere inside I was hurting. My eyes were moist, but I was proud of myself.

I was completely unsure of how I was going to start my apology, but nonetheless I was surely going to get through with it. I entered Jimmie's cafeteria and I looked at our spot.

Empty! It was empty! Dr. Fletcher was not there! I looked around to see if he was sitting at some other table. He wasn't there. I looked at my watch and the time was on my side. I was neither early, nor was I late. He should have been here like he always was.

Where was he?

CHAPTER THIRTEEN

LOST

I began to feel anxious for some reason. I had another good look at all the tables. I asked the lady at the counter, if she had seen the old man. She had no clue. My agitation rose by the minute. I went outside the cafeteria and began to wait for him to arrive. It grew darker and darker outside as the sun began to set, but there was no sign of him. It was at that moment that it occurred to me. I didn't even have his phone number; neither did I know where he lived. How could I have been so blunt? I finally decided to head back home, hoping that he would show up tomorrow.

I reached back home and gave my dad a call, to ask him how he was doing? I was obviously, not going to attend the funeral. That was still, too big a step for me to take. I preferred to mourn in silence and alone. But I just could not seem to get Dr. Fletcher's absence out of my mind. Why hadn't he showed up?

The following day, I went a couple of hours earlier, to ensure that I would not miss him. I sat there, sipping on my coffee, looking at the door every single time the bell at the door made a sound as a customer walked in, hoping it would be him.

Hours passed and he hadn't shown up.

I went back to the lady at the counter and asked her if she knew anything about him. She had absolutely no clue of who he was or where he lived. But she did tell me, after quite a bit of thinking, that a young lady would always bring him and later they would leave together.

Who was this girl? Why had he never mentioned her to me? Where was I going to find her? I continued to grow more anxious.

I had no address of him; I was ignorant enough to not even ask for his telephone number! His words of how people can be more self-involved that they think came whispering back to me. Two days passed and now I really started to lose my senses and I kept growing desperate by the hour. I sat in my room, feeling lost again. I so earnestly wanted to apologise to him. I wanted to know what had happened on the day of the phone call. I wanted to know what events lead him to be in the current state he was in. I wanted to know more about Emma and what her reply was!

But I had lost him. Maybe I was being a bit selfish, given the fact that I was mostly agitated because his story was left incomplete and his story was the driving source of inspiration to help me figure out mine.

I sat there, completely lost in thought and wondering what to do next. I went back to my study and sat there going through the various letters, notes and poems I had written. I looked through the notes that I had taken as I was conversing with Dr. Fletcher. Such beautiful words, I thought to myself and I flipped through the pages. His words were truly magical, filled with passion. And then, as I was reading through the words, my eyes got hooked onto something.

"12 C,
61 Oldham Street"

It was the address he had shouted while he was describing one of his incidents. This was something to begin. I started to smile, mostly because I had finally found an address to go to and get his story completed. I jumped with joy. I didn't care if I was being selfish. I needed that complete story of his. We always watch great romantic movies, listen to powerful romantic music, but no matter how much we are moved by them, we never really implement them in our lives. We convince ourselves saying that such things happen only in movies and we don't take them into considerations no matter how moving they are. But listening to a person and seeing their passion for love is something else. Yes, words can be misleading and can deceive. But in the case of Dr. Fletcher, he only narrated how he had lived his life, and how Emma had affected his life. It was I, who had attached greatness to his love for her. I needed this story so badly, for whatever reason it may be. I needed to get the whole story, in hopes that by the end of it, I would have all the answers I needed to progress in my own.

The next day, I got up all excited. I couldn't wait. My blood rushing through my veins and I could feel my heart thumping through my chest. The weather obviously was not on my side. It was pouring down like it always did, trying to make my condition worse like always.

Within an hour or so, I had reached the address. I stood there, looking at the green door that read "12 C." I walked up to the door and rang the bell. I stood there, my face beginning to smile as I could hear footsteps getting louder and louder.

The door clicked open and before standing, was the most beautiful girl I had ever laid my eyes upon. Her cheeks all pink, dimples appearing on her face as she smiled. Blue eyes, you could easily lose yourself in.

"May I help you?" she asked, finally breaking me from my over whelming feeling.

"Err, yes, I am looking for Dr. Fletcher. Is he home?" I asked. "Dr. Fletcher?" she asked looking confused. "I'm sorry sir, but there is no one here by that name. You must have gotten the wrong address" she replied.

"Dr. Aaron Fletcher! Long curly grey hair, rounded glasses, has a patchy beard, walks with a cane. Is this not his house?" I asked, beginning to get confused.

"No sir, there's no one here by that name" she persisted. "Have you seen the man I described around this neighbourhood?" I asked, refusing to give up. "We've been living here for quite some time sir and there are quite a few old couples living in this neighbourhood, but none of them seem to fit your descriptions" she said.

I was heartbroken. I was back to square one. I refused to give up. I went from door to door around the block, only to find nothing but bad news from each house. Where was he? Where did he go? As I walked back, I looked at the green door of 12 C one more time. I could picture a younger him running through that door towards his telephone to wait for the call. I could picture it so well. But where was he? Where was Dr. Aaron Fletcher?

It seemed to get darker around me by the minute; the day seemed to be coming to an end. I truly found myself to be completely lost.

CHAPTER FOURTEEN

A SELFISH THOUGHT

I sat by my fire place, heartbroken. Where do I find him? Where had he disappeared? My selfish thought continued to stay by my shoulders. It's not that I had no concern for his wellbeing; it's just that I needed that story for my own selfish needs. A human brain can do that to you at times. There's no denying the fact that no matter how nice, unconditional we try to be, deep down we have a selfish motive behind every action we perform.

At times, I question Dr. Fletcher's very existence. Did he even exist? Or was he just my own minds manifestation? Why was he nowhere to be found?

I could not sleep, for this night was cold. The cold kept me awake, but not alive. The only warm fire I had in my life was Rachel, whose fire kept diminishing as I spent every day away from her.

I thought of all the times I was selfish in my behaviour with Rachel. I remember this one night when I was being unreasonable and just refused to step out of my house as I was being haunted by some past memories of mine. I refused to pick up any calls and I just sat in my room. It had been two days since I had stepped out of home or gotten any sleep. That night, the doorbell rang and I remember vividly whining and crawling to the door. It was Rachel. She stood at my door with a smile. I remember just opening the door and walking back to my room, leaving the door open. It's not that I was not happy to see her; it's just that I didn't care much for why she was there. She followed me to my room. I just went and crashed on my bed and took my pillow and covered my face with it and just lay there. I didn't speak a word to her and neither did she. And then I heard her voice. She started to sing in a soft voice and I remember smiling vaguely under the pillow. Her voice grew louder and louder and I realised that she was walking closer to me and then she sat next to me. She gently lifted my head and put it on her lap and continued to sing. She hadn't even bothered to lift up the pillow as I held it to my face. She sang away the whole night and I do not remember the exact moment as to when I fell asleep. I remember waking up to her voice in the morning, she must have kept singing the whole time. I jumped out of the bed throwing the pillow and yelling out and asking her if she had any sleep the whole night. "No, my darling" she replied smiling.

I lost my nerve, "Why do you do this Rachel? I stayed away for two days because I didn't want anyone to be affected by me. I stayed away because I knew I can't let go of my demons and so I stayed by with them to ensure that they would not hurt anyone else. Why do you do this?" I shouted. "Now, don't you see that I have to carry this additional emotional baggage that you delivered to me last night and I cannot give this back to you" I added.

"You don't have to," she replied. "I did it for my own selfishness Sammy. I guess I just didn't want to be alone on my birthday and so I came over even though I knew you didn't want to see anyone. I am sorry for being so selfish" she added. She got up and walked out of my room with not an iota of anger or sadness in her face, apologising once again and she exited my room.

I stood there, completely agitated. What had just happened? Was she the one being selfish or was it me? There was no doubt, it was me! How could I have forgotten her birthday? How had I become so selfish? I truly had become a liability, both to myself and others!

And now here I was, still being the same selfish man I was. Selfishness need not always manifest evidently but if you look and search yourself deeply, you will realise how selfish you are as a person. I needed to find Dr. Fletcher for my own selfish emotional needs. Sadly, at the moment, my selfishness was the only thing I had with me to keep me going.

The next day, I went back to Jimmie's cafeteria, but this time I didn't even bother looking across the tables to our corner as I entered the cafeteria to see if he was there. Guess I was losing hope. I went to the counter, looking at the menu, trying to figure out what I wanted to order. The voices of the people had gotten louder just like before and it was irritating. "Hey boy!" a voice exclaimed. I looked up and it was the lady at the counter. "You kept asking me about the old man, right. Well he hasn't shown up, but the lady who he always leaves with, is here. I already told her that you have been asking about the old man since quite some time now. She's sitting over there" she said, pointing her finger to a figure. I looked back at the table and there she was, this blonde lady, sipping on her tea and reading the newspaper. I ran, towards the lady; I probably was afraid that even if I delayed myself by even a second, I would lose her.

"Hi! Do you know where Dr. Fletcher is?" I spoke out, without even an introduction, looking at her anxiously.

"Calm down, young man, I know where he is." She replied smiling. "Where is he? Where is Dr. Fletcher?" I asked growing even more anxious.

"He's at Jigsaw Independent Hospital, Palatine road, right here in Manchester" she replied trying to calm me. "He's in a hospital? Since when?" I asked, my confusion clearly beginning to manifest on my face.

"Since always!" she exclaimed. And then, again there was a silence I was unable to break.

'Since always,' what did she mean by that?

CHAPTER FIFTEEN

THE DAWN OF REALITY

I stood there in silence, in a state of shock. "Calm down son. There's nothing to worry about" the lady finally spoke breaking the silence. "Could you please take me to him ma'am? I need to see him" I told anxiously. She kindly obliged. Our ride in the taxi was just too surreal for me. I still could not believe that I was on my way to the hospital. "What happened to him?" I asked. "Well as of now, he's just suffering from a fractured ankle. About three days earlier, he struck himself with his cane out of anger. He does that at times. So, since he's unable to do a lot of walking, he just sits around in the hospital now" she said sighing.

Had he hit himself with the cane after our last confrontation? Were my words so hurtful? I began to feel the guilt build up in my veins and muscles. How could I have been so inconsiderate back then!

"It's all my fault! I exclaimed, covering my face with my hands out of guilt. "What do you mean?" she asked looking at me all confused. "The last time we met, we had an argument during which he really lost his temper and so did I. I told him things I didn't mean on sensitive issues which I knew would cause him pain. It was just in the heat of the moment, I didn't mean those things" I tried justifying myself to her.

"It's not your fault" she replied. "I mean, I understand why you would think it is your fault, and maybe you did act as a catalyst, but trust me when I tell you this, it's not your fault son" she said trying to console me. "He's always been self-destructive that way. This is not the first time he's hurt himself" she added. "What do you mean?" I asked, confused by her words.

"You remember I told you, he's been with us since a very long time. That's because he's suffering from a disease known as Korsakoff syndrome. He's been with us for quite some years now and I've been taking care of him for a while now. The hospital I'm taking you to right now, is a mental health institution which supports people with mental disorders. At Jigsaw Independent Hospital, we use the 'recovery model' and the 'valuing people' principles to provide a range of active rehabilitation and treatments to help our patients."

I was still in a state of shock. I was unable to digest any of the things she was telling me.

"What do you mean by mental illness? Are you telling me that he's crazy?" I asked, cutting her mid-sentence, growing anxious by the minute.

"Not exactly, but he has lost quite a bit of memory. He's unable to recollect recent incidents and people. His past is a complete puzzle to figure out. He may not even remember you" she said.

By now, we had reached the hospital and I just had to get away from all this information I was being given.

"Could you please stop!" I exclaimed. "Just take me to him please, I want to see him and talk to him" I said, my voice beginning to crack by now.

I followed her quietly without uttering a single word. I could not believe it when she told me that, he would not remember me. I refused to accept it and I was sure, after all the conversations we had, he would definitely remember me. He just had to.

We reached this backyard and I saw a bunch of people sitting around, walking and laughing. And then, I saw him, sitting on a chair under the shade of a tree, reading something. He had that smile that he wore every time we met. He seemed like the happy Dr. Fletcher I knew. I began to smile and I walked up to him.

"Hello Dr. Fletcher, how are you?" I asked. He looked up and into my eyes and smiled. It seemed so familiar, and then he finally spoke.

"It almost feels like it's the 16thof July, doesn't it. I can feel her close by!"

Every muscle in my body went weak. It had been 4 days since our last meet and the last time we had met, was on the 16thof July. I could not come to terms with this. "No sir, it's the 20thof July!" I exclaimed looking at him anxiously. "Ah yes, no wonder her fragrance is still around the corner" he replied.

With every sentence he spoke, my heart began to pound harder and harder. Where was the Dr. Fletcher I knew?

"Do you know who I am Dr. Fletcher?" I asked, praying from within, hoping that he would recognise me. He gave a hard stare and then smiled and told, "You do look very familiar. Are you one of those kids who visit us every week and does all the paintings? You are, aren't you? I must admit, I really loved your work."

My heart broke into a thousand pieces. He didn't know me. Let's put aside the fact that he did not remember the last fight we had and the things I told him, he did not even know who I was!

My eyes filled with tears and I just turned around and walked away.

I felt a gentle tug on my shoulder as I walked away. It was the lady who had brought me to him.

"Don't cry, I know it's hard for you to digest these facts all at once" she said trying to comfort me.

"But he does not even recognise me!" I shouted unable to contain my emotions.

CHAPTER SIXTEEN

ANONYMOUS TEARS

I was unable to contain my emotions and broke into the arms of this stranger in front of me. She didn't say a word; she just took me in her arms and let me cry my heart out. Why was I so affected by this? Who was Dr. Fletcher to me? What was this bond that I had created with him? Was I hurting because I felt like I had lost someone or was I hurting because I had emotionally invested myself into nothingness?

"Please tell me what is wrong with him" I said, getting a hold of myself. She walked me to one of the benches and we both took a seat with Dr. Fletcher directly in my line of vision and I couldn't help but notice how happy he looked.

"He was brought to us many years back; I had not been working in this hospital back then. He was brought due to severe mental derailment which was probably due to all his severe alcohol abuse. If he had been brought to us sooner, we probably could have reversed the effects of the disease, but now it's past that point and it does not seem to be reversible. "Alcohol abuse? What do u mean?" I asked. "Well he had a long history of alcohol abuse which is probably what caused him to suffer from this disease. He must have gotten hooked to it at a very early age. He's got vague memory of recent events, but has quite a few of past events stored quite well in him. He also suffers from a certain degree of confabulation."

"Confabulation? I don't understand!" I exclaimed interrupting her. "Well confabulation is a case wherein the person's mental abilities is severely disorganised. They produce a lot of fabricated, distorted, or misinterpreted memories about themselves or the world, without the conscious intention to deceive."

"Emma!" I shouted. She was the first thing that came popped in my head.

"Well I see that he has spoken about Emma to you too, well she's the only person he speaks about pretty much to everyone" she replied.

"Did he make her up? Does she not exist?" I shouted looking at Dr. Fletcher who was just sitting there, all calm, just reading to himself.

"Calm down, son." she replied trying to calm my agitation. "To be brutally honest with you, I really don't know. He's told me quite a bit of stories and incidents when I continued to ask him leading questions. He mixes up a lot of incidents. He has forgotten quite a bit of his past and he does make up quite a bit of interesting stories of recent times which I know are clearly made up."

Her words were striking down on me like million bolts of lightings.

"You remember he asked you if you were one of the kids who come here every week with the paintings" she said.

My eyes lowered down because I knew where she was going with this. "Well, we never had any kids come down here with paintings!"

I grew emotionally weaker with every word she said.

"But, he spoke to me every day, we spoke every day. He knew me. We would start off from where we had stopped!" I exclaimed trying to deny the truth, both to her and myself.

She again smiled and I had started to get annoyed by how calm she was being about all these things. But then, she had been dealing with it for a couple of years now.

"Well think back son! Did he ever address you by your name? Did he ever start a conversation with you?"

I thought back, I thought back hard and then it dawned on me. It was I who had always initiated conversation and as for addressing me, he never did actually address me by name. My head dropped.

"He must have addressed you, but only by vague terms such as boy, son or something like that, always general terms" she said.

It really hit me hard by now, what I thought was a sign of his care when he referred to me as 'son,' or 'boy' or even 'fool' for that matter was nothing but a sign of non-recognition of who I really was.

"But he spoke to me every day, he spoke so kindly. He narrated his story to me like he knew me, everyday" I shouted back refusing to accept the truth. "That's the thing about them" she replied.

"They are unaltered by behaviour. He must have just propagated what you initiated. If he, by character was a very outgoing person and comfortable talking to any number of people at any given time, he would continue to do so because their personality for that matter remains unaffected. That's why, more often than not, the other person usually fails to even notice the issue at hand" she added, trying to give me a clearer idea as to what he was suffering from and more importantly trying to help me accept the situation.

I looked at him one more time, and this time, he seemed like a completely different person.

"For what it's worth son, as for the part of Emma, I feel she's true. He's been so persistent about her. His facts about her, do not seem to change no matter how many times he tells it" she said trying to comfort me.

I guess she had figured out that their story was something I was holding on to.

"What about his friends, his family?" I asked. "Well, I guess they did visit him in the earlier years, but now I guess, they've all accepted the situation and moved on with their lives because they know he's safe here and meeting him and talking to him probably only gives them more pain" she said.

"So they just left him here, alone with his thoughts" I said to her with tears flowing uncontrollably, refusing to stop even for a second.

"People are selfish that way!" she said with a smile. "People tend to choose themselves over everyone else, eventually. Life is a harsh truth son; we have to accept it eventually."

Her words completely silenced me, because I knew she was right and the bottom line was, I was being selfish too, feeding off his story in an attempt to find solutions for my own.

"What about Emma?" I asked.

"I don't know!" she replied. "It's been so many years now, I don't know where his friends are, to even ask about her. But after I have come here and been appointed to take care of him, no woman with that name has ever come to visit him. I don't know if she exists, but my heart wants to believe that she did" she said.

"Does" I shouted correcting her. "Dr. Fletcher hates it when you refer to her in the past tense. She does exist. I don't care what you have to say." I shouted with a breaking voice.

"I need some time to get out of all this and accept these facts" I said getting up, wiping my tears.

"I understand. Take your time. You know where to find us. Just ask for me when you visit us next time, my name is Stacy Brown."

I thanked her for everything and walked away without looking back at Dr. Fletcher. Emotional Hell was too small a term to describe what I was feeling.

CHAPTER SEVENTEEN

ACCEPTANCE

How was I going to face a tomorrow with this truth in my heart? Was it all a lie? Was Emma just a figment of his imagination? No matter, how much I wanted to believe that he was telling the truth, I just could not help but think to myself of the other alternative. If she was just a creation of his, there was nothing special to his story anymore. All that I had learnt, for some reason, felt useless. Story telling has no greatness in it. For, most of it, I thought it was pathetic. It's not that I had not imbibed certain qualities in myself from the conversations that I had with Dr. Fletcher. It's just that we are inspired by stories of reality, not fiction. Yes, we can take in certain aspects from everything we hear and see, but how much of it do we actually accept and take? I needed this eternal story to be true, to help teach me the values of human emotions. Call it arrogance, but if this story were false, I would discard it completely and it would be nothing but saw dust to me.

I decided to confront him again the next day. I knew, conversations with him would not get me any closer to the truth, but I had no other choice. Fake or not, I had to know his story. I had to know what had happened on the day of the phone call. I gathered up all my strength and decided that I would ask him about Emma. I had no more patience in me, to listen to details.

The following day, I went back to the hospital and saw so many people, of varied ages all involved in some recreational activities. The hospital, tries to create an environment excelling in rehabilitation and human confrontation. Stacy would take Dr. Fletcher to the cafeteria every day for the very same reason, where I was unfortunate enough to have met him. Why did I have this sudden resentment towards him? I kept asking myself.

I walked up to him, as he sat there, by the tree looking at other people having their walks and listening to all the people around him talk. "Hello Dr. Fletcher how's your leg now" I asked wearing a fake smile. "It's all right, I feel much better today son" he replied. I just wanted to cut the conversation to as short as possible. "Tell me about the phone call Dr. Fletcher" I said, with no hesitation whatsoever. I guess, by now, I had made peace with the fact that he was mentally unwell. I just wanted to know more about the story and I wanted to know what had happened. Now when I think back, I realise how truly selfish and obsessed I was. But I guess, these raw emotions are really our primary nature and no matter what we do, we cannot overcome them.

He just sat there, smiling. Before he could ask me, if it was the 16th of July, I asked him again.

"What about Emma's phone call Dr. Fletcher?"

"Ah, yes! I had asked her to give me a call on the 6th of January, irrespective of what she had to say. I waited every day, like a fool. I remember, storming into the house, throwing my coat on the floor, taking my right as swiftly as I could and running upstairs and running into my room which was straight down the hallway bursting open the door and staring at my telephone which was in the corner of the room. My telephone lay brightly lit in the corner with light. The light from my window opposite was obstructed by huge branches from a tree outside and the light would fall perfectly, only on half of the wall, the side which had the telephone. Bless that tree!" he exclaimed.

"Dr. Fletcher!" I shouted, interrupting him midway, realising that he was repeating what he had already told me before. "I know, you kept looking at your watch, then you would close your eyes and wait for the phone call, only to realise that it never happened! You've told me this before!" I said, shouting as I spoke, out of frustration.

"I have? When? Oh wait, did we meet at the park the other day? You were with a friend, weren't you?"

"NO, I was not!" I shouted trying to keep my nerve. "The phone call, tell me what happened on the day of the phone call, on January 6th. What did Emma tell you?" I asked growing more agitated.

He just paused, he lowered his head and began to nod and mumbled something to himself. I tried to hear what he was trying to say to me.

"I beg your pardon?"

More whispering answers continued from his side. "Dr. Fletcher, what did Emma tell you?" I asked.

"Dr. Fletcher..."

"I don't know!" he shouted. "I don't know. I was not at home on January 6th. I did not hear the phone ring." He said breaking down.

"What do you mean you weren't home? Where did you go? What happened?," waiting for him to give an answer. "I don't know," he shouted. "I can't remember. I needed milk. Milk, I went out to get some milk" he continued trying to explain the whole situation.

"What happened then?" I asked, hoping that he would suddenly get all the answers which I knew was impossible.

"I don't know" he said, breaking down completely.

I just sat there, continuing to look at him break down. How could he not remember? How could he remember vivid details of certain incidents and lose out whole days of memories of the other.

"Did Emma come to meet you after that?" I asked hoping he would give me an answer. "I don't know!" was his reply yet again.

Silence, was all we had between us yet again, but this time it was a different kind of silence. It felt strange and unknown to me.

Did he even live the life, he claimed he did?

CHAPTER EIGHTEEN

SELF CONFRONTATION

I needed answers. Not for the sake of Dr. Fletcher, not for Rachel. I needed them for me. Everything I had begun to believe, everything I started to realise, somehow felt pointless without the reality of Dr. Fletcher's story. I needed this reality check, that in this world filled with misery, there are people who stand by what they feel with no regrets. People with no fear of outcomes, or endings, who are able to stare into the unknown and keep moving forwards with hope in their hearts, filling it with nothing but love. It seemed too good to be true for a reality, and the fact that Dr. Fletcher was living it, made me believe otherwise. But now, after what had happened in the past few days, I think to myself of why the reality of the story is so crucial. Beliefs and actions are two completely different things. Us believing in some action and us actually doing it, have a difference as gross as the sea and the sky, both are limitless but completely different. Believing you are in love and putting the mental effort is one entity, but letting the mental effort manifest as a physical entity, through words, actions, patience is something else.

I kept re-reading his words from the things I had written down during our conversations. My eyes could not help but evade the address he had given me. He could not have made that up. He could have fictionalised his stories and emotions, but not the address. It was too precise to have been made up. His descriptions of the house were too vivid to be imaginary. I decided to pay a visit to the house one more time. The clouds were fast filling the sky with thunder beginning to rumble, I didn't care much for the weather anymore.

I stood there, outside the door of 12 C. My mind kept picturing a younger Dr. Fletcher running every afternoon to wait for a phone call which he knew wouldn't come that day. I rang the doorbell and waited. For some reason, I kept picturing myself to be in Dr. Fletcher's shoes. The door opened to the same familiar strange face.

"Hello, I'm Sam Gray, we met a couple of days ago. I came here looking for someone" I said. The lady took a few seconds to place me, but eventually did. "Oh yes, I remember. How may I help you?" she asked.

"I need to have a look at your house if you don't mind!" I said and the lady gave me the most confused look and began to close to the door, clearly disapproving.

"Ma'am please, wait!" I exclaimed, holding the door.

To this day, I can't remember what my words were. I just went on talking and trying to explain the best of what I could make of the situation. I had no definite cause as to why I wanted to see the house, but something in me told me that, this house is the only explanation, I could ever have. After a lot of talking and hand gestures and head scratching and teary eyes of mine, to my surprise, the lady stopped me midway and obliged. To this day, I do not know what made her do that.

As I entered the house, Dr. Fletcher's voice continued to echo in my head. I looked to the left and I could see his wet coat on the floor even though it wasn't there. As I walked, I could hear his footsteps as he ran through the hallway. I took the right and there it was, a staircase and all I could see was an anxious Dr. Fletcher run up these stairs only to fall down again. As I walked up these stairs, my eyes began to blur out from the tears I was trying to hold in. I looked to the end of the hallway, and there it was! A door! I walked slowly towards it, his footsteps getting louder in my head. My trembling hands held the door knob and I took in a deep breath and I opened the door. The room looked so different than I had imagined. There were toys, a bed and books all over. It was probably the lady's son's room. I looked to the corner and saw nothing. It was an empty corner. There was a giant clock in the room and I looked at it. It was nearing 3:15 PM. I could picture him here. I could feel his solitude and yearnings. Then something happened, the clouds suddenly broke away and the sunlight passed through and the window and about half of the wall lit up. I could not believe my eyes and I looked out of the window and there it was, the branches of the tree.

He was here, this was his room! I walked up to the corner and I could see the telephone now. I could see the jar by it with lilies. I could see Dr. Fletcher sitting on the bed with eyes closed waiting like a fool for that phone call. I could finally see it all, he truly had done it.

The Dr. Fletcher I knew, was real and his love truly was everlasting.

I fell to my knees and for the first time, my legs had lost their strength not because they were weak, but because I had just found the most beautiful thing filling up my heart. The power of love and its effects began to shine like a thousand rays of light overpowering all the darkness I had within.

The baggage I seemed to be carrying finally seemed to have fallen off. This man lives every day staring into the unknown. I can only imagine the level of anxiety he would have been feeling everyday. But he chose to think of all the wonderful things about Emma and made sure that his heart continued to beat for her till this very day.

Somehow, knowing all this, it gave me all the closure that I ever needed. Maybe I found myself to be very similar to Dr. Fletcher in more ways than I could imagine and I knew that I had this chance of correcting myself and making myself a better person and not lose it all by carrying this fear of the future. The leap of faith he had taken gave me the strength to take mine. I guess the greatest love story one ever knows will be the one they lived. I was ready to live my story.

I was ready to take my leap of faith!

CHAPTER NINETEEN

THE DECISION

My mind, as I walked back from the house, was absolutely clear. For the first time, in a really long time, I felt so wonderfully happy. I went back to the hospital and I went to Dr. Fletcher's room. He sat there on a chair, busy writing in his book.

"Hello, Dr. Fletcher, how are you today?" I asked. He looked up and smiled, and it was the same smile that he always gave me. I guess it was just my perception of the smile that made the difference. The smile felt strange when I thought of him to be a stranger who didn't know me and now, it went back to being familiar, like before because I had come to know him.

"Oh, I'm doing good son. It's just that my foot hurts sometimes, but I'm good otherwise" he said.

It no longer mattered to me to find out what happened on the day of the phone call, all that mattered to me was to know if the story he told me was true and today I had gotten the answer to my satisfaction. I couldn't help but notice his book, it had a lot of descriptions of various people he had met and the date was marked as today.

"What's in the book sir?" I asked. "Oh, it's just random things I write from day to day and the people I meet. It helps me they say" he said.

I suddenly remembered that, he had scribbled down things after each meet of ours.

Just as I was about to ask him to flip back a few pages and ask him to read what he had written about me, I was stopped by my own thoughts.

Why did I need it? Why do we need to know every single detail of emotions and thoughts? Why was it necessary for me to know what he thought about me? It was not!

I just smiled and got down on my knees and gave him a hug without saying a single word. I didn't want to let go for some reason and I could feel his arms getting tighter around me. I guess, he wanted that hug too; at least I tell myself that. That day, as I hugged him, I could feel my granddad all around me; his essence was truly magical that night.

I bid goodbye and I left the hospital.

I chose to walk back home that night and it was raining heavily, but I didn't care. My mind and heart was filled with happiness and I thought to myself, what is love?

What is love?

A question often asked by almost all of us, and more often than not, asked by the same individual at different stages of his or her life.

Is love the connection we feel when we look at someone for the first time and have butterflies in our stomach and palpitations in our heart, or is love the feeling of calmness and peace when we look into the person's eyes for the first time?

Is love the connections we make with a person, which lead us to have expectations from them or is love the bonds we make with people who are no longer living wherein there is no scope for any expectations?

Is love the feeling of closeness with someone who is far away, or is it the feeling of feeling distanced from someone who is in front of us?

Is love the laughter and smiles we wear when we think about a person, or is love the tears that roll down our cheeks when we think about another heart?

Is love seeing a smile on your face when you look into the mirror, thinking of someone else, or is it trying to put a smile on another's face when they are feeling low?

Is love the anxiety and fear we feel when we think about someone or is it the feeling of strength and courage we receive thinking about them?

So what is it?

It's so simple to understand and yet so complex to determine.

Love is all of these things and, at the same time, none of these things! Love is, and always has been a subjective emotion and never an objective one The day, the world defines love, will be the day we can say for sure that love no longer exists!

I knew one thing for sure, as I walked back home. It was that I was madly and completely in love with Rachel and Dr. Fletcher had taught me through his life that if the game at hand is love, then we just put in all our thoughts, emotions, work, life and everything we hold dear in it. We live by it, and stand by it, irrespective of what the world has to say to us. Those who love, do not need sympathy, they don't need condolences, for love is a privilege and not a burden.

Dr. Fletcher could have held anything close to his heart, may it be the day of January 6th, the day of departure. But every time, we met, he asked me if it was the 16th of July, the day he first met Emma Veaton, and I think that says a lot about him as a person. He chose to remember the days that made him happy rather than the days that put him down. He didn't think of his story as an inspiration, he didn't preach it out as a lesson, he simply expressed it day in and out keeping it as simple as the breaths we take. It was his necessity and the greatest lesson that I learnt from him was that all stories start out as just stories, it is we who have to bring in the greatness to it.

I reached home that night and I stood by the phone. I was soaking wet and the water kept dripping down from my hair onto the phone and it almost felt like the first time Dr. Fletcher had called Emma, the feeling was surreal.

I picked up the phone, without a doubt in my mind, I felt ready, I felt in love and it was the helpless love I used to feel for Rachel. This was a love of give and take and I was ready for it in every way possible.

'Tring tring!'
"Tring tring!'
"Hello!"
"Hello Rachel, it's me!"
"Sammy!"
"How are you?"........

CHAPTER TWENTY

Privileged Emotions

Life soon got calm, calm as a sea breeze. Rachel and I got back together and she did take her time to accept me, for what I had become. For the most part, she could not believe it. Love is strange that way, but that's alright. I guess that's the beauty of love, it's like a masterpiece of abstract art. It's so subjective that the definition of it changes from person to person. She did eventually forgive me and accept me and more importantly I did the same for myself. One thing that I have learnt is that, life is nothing, but a prisoner of time. The small wonderful moments we have with our special ones, is the closest thing we can have to freedom. Let us not lose these moments and live the rest of our lives in regret.

I told her all about Dr. Fletcher and she was so moved by it all, that she begged me to take her to him. We would visit him, every week and it didn't matter to me anymore, if he recognised me or not, the important fact was that he taught me lessons without which I would not have become the person I am today. I am not as sure as to if his love was an untouched love, but I do know that it will be a love untouched.

He did get worse as time progressed and his health deteriorated drastically and I and Rachel went through it all, she more than me, being the wonderful person she is. We did eventually get married and it was one of the most beautiful decisions of my life. Yes, we have our ups and downs, the downs more likely to be caused by me, but I guess I'm finally not afraid to let Rachel help me back on my feet and it feels good to know that every emotion can be shared with another person and it truly does make life a better place and you truly begin to appreciate the little things in life.

I still remember the day of his funeral, I watched them lower his casket and I stood there with a fist full of mud and as I dropped the mud onto his casket, I remembered his words, and I knew for sure, that this mud, would stick to his casket and the earth would accept him for his heart had nothing but love for Emma. His story will forever remain eternal, because it lives in me and I shall pass it on, to Rachel and the wonderful two kids that I have right now, Aaron and Arya, whose voices fill my heart with peace and make me proud of every single decision that I ever took, the good and the bad ones.

I sit here, twenty years down the line, penning down pieces of my emotions, not to convey any message to the world. Perhaps I just needed an outlet for all the wonderful emotions that I have within me which were nurtured over time with patience and love and warmth by wonderful people around me and in the process, probably my words will reach out to a young boy in Amsterdam who sets right the raincoat of his girlfriend or probably a lost teenager in India trying to figure out his emotions or to a young girl in USA, who sits and contemplates her decisions of life. I am perhaps selfish that way, but I guess all humans are. I truly believe that if the roots of our selfishness does good to others in some way, then I think that's the most wonderful way of expressing selfless love.

Love is like the air we breathe, we do not always take notice of it, but it's there all around us, protecting us and now I know for a fact that love does not kill, it keeps you alive and I truly believe that with all my heart and soul.

As for Emma Veaton, EV, his sunshine as he called her, I'll choose to keep her forever immortalised just the way Dr. Fletcher had described her, perfect in every way possible. She could have been nothing like how Dr. Fletcher had explained perhaps. She could have been a completely different person from how he described her and probably caused him more pain than happiness in someone else's perspective. But it does not matter, because Dr. Aaron Fletcher believed that she was the most beautiful girl he had met and that's all that mattered. Everyone and everything else, all the other opinions are just peripherals and meaningless. I guess this cynical world could use a little bit of perfection and I choose to keep that perfection as the image of Emma as described by Dr. Fletcher.

I do not know what happened on the January 6th, why he didn't make it home, if Emma called or not and where was she all this while. But that's ok, the essence of this story will forever be entrenched in me and I shall keep this essence with me only to pass it to another.

Love needs to touch us just once and its effects can remain untouched for a lifetime.

Love truly is a privilege and not a burden.

CHAPTER TWENTY-ONE

REALITY OF JANUARY 6TH

The sun shines bright outside 12 C, 61 Wellfield road, Manchester. There is no coat by the door this afternoon; the house seems more silent that it usually does. The clock ticks, closer and closer towards 2:45 PM. The room seems calm and silent, but oddly weird without the anxiously waiting person in the room. The sunlight falls perfectly on the wall like it always does. The vase by the telephone still has the same flowers from the previous day. They are not replaced.

The clock ticks closer and closer to 2:45 PM.

2:44 and 55 seconds, 56, 57, 58, 59, 60.

2:45 and 1, 2, 3, 4....

'Tring tring'

'Tring tring'

THE END

Printed in Great Britain
by Amazon